NOW WE ARE
SIX HUNDRED

BBC

DOCTOR WHO
NOW WE ARE
SIX HUNDRED

James Goss

Illustrations by Russell T Davies

HARPER
DESIGN
An Imprint of HarperCollins Publishers

Doctor Who: Now We Are Six Hundred
Text © copyright 2017 by James Goss
Illustrations © copyright 2017 by Russell T Davies

HarperCollins books may be purchased for educational, business,
or sales promotional use. For information please email the Special Markets
Department at SPsales@harpercollins.com.

Published in 2017 by
Harper Design
An Imprint of HarperCollins*Publishers*
195 Broadway
New York, NY 10007
Tel: (212) 207-7000
Fax: (855) 746-6023
harperdesign@harpercollins.com
www.hc.com

Distributed throughout the world by
HarperCollins Publishers
195 Broadway
New York, NY 10007

Doctor Who is a BBC Wales production for BBC One.
Executive producers: Steven Moffat and Brian Minchin

Editorial Director: Albert DePetrillo
Editor: Charlotte Macdonald
Copyeditor: Steve Tribe
Production: Alex Merrett

Library of Congress Control Number: 2017932198

ISBN 978-0-06-268539-1

Printed and bound in the United States of America
First Printing, 2017

CONTENTS

BEFORWARDS

Dawn came to the Thousand Year Wood. It had snowed again, as it always did. Figment poked his head out of his little burrow and made his careful way through the fresh white snow.

He wondered if today he'd meet Whoot the Owl. Whoot had been working on a Special Snowing Song, the words of which he'd learned by heart yesterday, but today they were gone from the tip of his tongue.

"Oh dear," said Figment. "I must stop keeping things on the tip of my tongue."

He carried on his happy way through the Thousand Year Wood, trying ever so hard to remember that song. Songs were like that in the Thousand Year Wood. You'd go to sleep with them laid out ready to slip on the next morning, only to wake up and find them all covered in the snow of a new day.

Figment wondered which of his friends he'd find in the snow today. Perhaps TymeWore (such a sad little donkey) or maybe he'd be whisked away by Dr Roo, who'd want him to go hunting for Gallifrump.

Figment pottered on, until he stubbed his toe against something in the snow.

"Ow," said Figment and scratched his head when he'd stopped rubbing his toe. "What's this?"

It was a tree, hidden in the snow. He worked to uncover it, singing a jolly little Uncovering Song as he worked. The tree was square and blue, which was exciting, as Figment had never seen a blue tree before. There was some writing on the blue tree, which Figment couldn't quite make out. He scratched his head (which had seen a good deal of scratching) and spelt out what he could.

"OFFICERSANDCARS
RESPOND TO URGENT CALLS"

Figment read it again and he smiled. "How terribly nice of Officer Sandcars," he said to himself. Figment wondered ever so much what he looked like.

"I do hope my call is urgent," said Figment. "Or, at least, that it sounds urgent."

Puzzling this problem, Figment wandered away into the Thousand Year Wood. He was humming to himself, humming a tune which the strange blue tree had taught him...

FULL STOP

(*after* 'The End')

When I was One
I was not much fun

When I was Two
I was barely through

When I was Three
I liked strong tea

When I was Four
I hated a bore

When I was Five
I was so alive

When I was Six
I somehow could never quite fit in to what was
expected of me, well, not exactly but that was
because things weren't neat and there are no
easy rhymes in the universe and scansion, my
dear Peri, is a thing that's really overrated and
you only have to look at a sunset to realise that
creation itself is a poem and oh no wait, got it,
of course, *Fix*! The line needed to end with *Fix*!
(Or *tricks*. That works too.)

When I was Seven
I sent gods to Heaven

When I was Eight
Kissing was great

When I was Nine
I fought time

When I was Ten
I began again

When I was Eleven
I totally got even

When I was Twelve, I became as clever as clever
And now I think I'll be Twelve for ever and ever*

(*Unless, of course, there is a terrible catastrophe involving explosions, radiation or heights. And then I guess we'll find out what comes next. But the eyebrows won't be as good.)

CONSULTATION
EXERCISE

(*after* 'Disobedience')

"Quarks, Quarks
Cybermen, Cybermen
Mechonoids, Voord, Zarbi
Take great care!" said the Doctor
"Although I am only me.
It's more than it's worth to invade the Earth, without
First consulting me."

"Quarks, Quarks
Cybermen, Cybermen
Mechonoids, Voord, Zarbi
If your Battlefleet happens to
In the vicinity be
Then I'll teach you – reluctantly"
(said the Dr, said he)
"To give the Earth a rather wide berth, rather
Than tangle with me."

Davros
Put up a notice
"WANTED DEAD or ALIVE!
(BEST DEAD)
THIS NASTY IMPOSTOR
THAT SOME CALL THE DOCTOR
JUST CANNOT BE SHOWN TO THRIVE
(PS: DO LEAVE OFF THE EARTH, IT'S REALLY
OUR TURF, AND WELL,
WE WOULD SO HATE TO FIGHT)."

Quarks, Quarks
Cybermen, Cybermen
Mechonoids, Voord, Zarbi
They all took some exception
To this unkind direction.
"So that is how old man Davros
Thinks it is going to be?
To tell us the Earth is his private turf? The cheek
Of the man. Well, we'll see."

Quarks, Quarks
Cybermen, Cybermen
(Commonly known as Them)
Told their friends, relations and alien nations
That, well
Sol 3 was a bit of a gem.
"We'll conquer the Earth for all that it's worth. But first
We'll give Davros something to see."

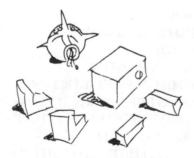

Quarks, Quarks,
Many and all and each
Got up a peach of a fleet
With which
Davros a lesson to teach,
But sadly themselves overreached.
And the battle's too grim to repeat.
Save that
Ev'ron's plans for the Earth, no matter their worth, ended
In total defeat.

"Q. Q.
C. C.
M. V. & ZB!"
Said the Dr (Commonly known as He)
"Oh dear
Oh dear and oh dear me
I told you so and that was my plea.
This is what happens you see.
It is more than it's worth to invade the Earth, without
First consulting me."

DALEK

(*after* 'Furry Bear')

If I were a Dalek
And a big Dalek too
I shouldn't much care
If it froze or snew.

I shouldn't much mind
If it rained acid
I'd be all lead-lined
With a coat like his.

For I'd have no eyes just a stalk to see
And I'd have no legs but I'd glide nicely
There'd be no arms but my big gun would kill
And there'd be a sucker which would, um, still-
I would have no heart and I'd have no soul
Which would help when being lonely takes its toll.

If I were a Dalek
And a big Dalek too
I shouldn't much care
What happened to you.

You could run away
You could say goodbye
And I'd be all lead-lined
With a coat like his.

TAKING THE AIR

(after 'Sand-between-the-toes')

There was a roaring in the sky
The pigeons cried as they blew by
We tried to talk but had to shout
Someone had let the Atmos out.

Air is lovely, air is clean
Life without is jolly mean.

Sontarans are boist'rous fellows
If a trifle 'clined to bellow.
Why they've stol'n the air I've no idea
But it makes living tricky here.

The sky is nice, the sky is blue
But right now it's choking too.

Nanny says best not to worry
Just hold on tight, don't you hurry.
The Doctor, he will sort it out
So she was taught and has no doubt.

It's getting dark, it's getting dire-
Good Lord! And now the sky's on fire!

Doctor, Doctor, do please hurry
Nanny has begun to worry.
Big Ted's gone quiet – it's his last breath
I fear we may now choke to

RETIRING

(*after* 'Knight-in Armour')

On days I don't want to Doctor much
I worry that I shall lose my touch
All that running down those corridors
Thwartings of tyrants and dreadful bores
Brave rescues from the Foul Monster's Lair
And firm trouncing all the Demons There.

Chaos never ends, oh that's the shame
So yes I tire of just one more game.
Sometimes when the same old fight begins
I fear, just once, I'll let Evil win.
And then, on second thought, perhaps I won't
Because they're Monsters, and so I don't.
On days like that I don't think at all
That being the Doctor's so bad after all.

WAITING FOR
A FRIEND

(*after* 'Rice Pudding')

"What is the matter with Sarah Jane?
She stands and stands out in the rain.
Let's just ask, for sure she'll tell
I do not think that she looks well…"

Owl and I
I and Owl
Wait for a friend
Who never comes.

(Well, not yet)

Yes, he did not come today
But he'll surely come tomorrow.

Maybe he came last Wednesday week?
Oh, that'd be a sorrow.

Owl and I
I and Owl
Waiting for a friend
Who never comes.

Don't you worry –
It's just like HIM
"I'll not forget you."
(All toothy grin)

I'm quite sad,
My brain's disordered
I'm sure it's NOT
What the Doctor ordered.

The cheek!
The nerve!

He dumps me here,
Sight unseen
In holy, roly, poly
Aberdeen!!!

No, he did not come today.
No, will not come tomorrow.
He did not come last Wednesday week.
Face it, girl.
Oh, and-
Bus fare borrow.

"What was the matter with Sarah Jane?
She no longer stands out in the rain.
She smiles and smiles and won't say why
There's that odd look in her eye."

Owl and I
I and Owl
Waited for a friend.
Who never came.

CONTENTS

(after 'Happiness')

The Doctor
Had
A nice
New face.

It fitted
Well.
Went
Into place.

The hair was
Short.
The nose just
Right.

The legs were
Firm.
The eyes quite
Bright.

The problem
Was:
"These clothes
Won't Do!"

"They're off-the-
Peg
I'll have something
New!"

"A frilly
Shirt?"
(Think I'm over them)

"Time for a
Scarf?"
(A touch too soon)

"Some sturdy
Boots!"
(Handy for the moon)

"And finally
A nice new
Hat."

"And that,"
(said the Doctor)
"Is that."

DEAR HUMANS

What a funny little planet
All green and blue
And what funny people in it
Including you.

A few million years since you crawled
Up out the mud,
Looked at the skies and how they called
It's in your blood.

An inventive, invincible
Curious species.
Yet destructive, stupid, cruel.
How odd truth is.

You've cosmic wars and holocausts
Fought and survived.
Flood, famine, solar flares and plague
Suffered through, thrived.

You're puny defenceless bipeds
Homo Sapiens.
Yet wonderfully tough, I've said.
(I'm man's best friend.)

For here is the human spirit
Undoubtedly.
Amongst the stars, ready to outsit
Eternity.

Indomitable!
In
  dom
     it
       able!

THE DEATH LIST

(after 'The King's Breakfast')

The King asked
The Queen and
The Queen asked
The Chamberlain
"Could we have the Doctor made
So very very dead?"
The Queen asked
The Chancellor.
The Chancellor
Said "Certainly
I'll go and talk to
The People
Now
Before they go to bed."

The Chancellor
He exited
And went and told
The Alderman
"Don't forget the Doctor must
be very nicely dead."
The Alderman told
The Vizier
The Vizier
Said "Certainly
I'll go and talk to
The Prime Minister
Before she goes to bed."

The Prime Minister
Said "I hear you"
And went and told
The Guard Captain
"His Majesty would like the Doctor
To be swiftly, neatly dead."
The Guard Captain told
The Henchmen
The Henchmen
They said "Obviously,
We'll go and tell
The Assassin
Before they go to bed."

The Henchmen
They nodded
And went and told
The Assassin
"Don't forget you'd better make
the Doctor very, very dead."
The Masked Assassin
Said slyly
"You'd better tell
His Majesty
That many people nowadays
Like democracy
Instead."

The King said
"Bother!"
And then he said
"Democracy?"
The King sobbed. "Oh infamy!"
And went back to bed.
"Nobody,"
He whimpered
"Could call me
A nasty man.
I only want
Eternal rule
And the Doctor dead."

The Queen said
"There! There!"
And went and told
The Chancellor.
The Chancellor
Said "There! There!"
And went to the people.
The people said
"There! There!
We didn't really mean it.
We're happy in our misery
Take the Doctor in our stead."

The Queen took
The Doctor
And brought her to
His Majesty.
The King said
"Doctor, eh?"
And he bounded out of bed.
(And the Doctor smiled

Quietly)
"You know
I was your Masked Assassin.
Fraid you'll have to do the job
Of killing me instead."

The King said
"Nobody
Could call me
A fussy man.
But must I be the one
to make the Doctor dead?"
The Doctor said
"Certainly.
I've emptied out your slave mines
And your guards they have all fled.
The people
Have spoken
They're on their way
With pitchforks
AND
I think you'd better try exile instead…"

SPECIAL
FEATURES

Do you suppose
An Adipose
Nose
Grows and Grows
The more that it Knows?

*

Do you think
An Angel
Shrinks
When it Blinks?

I really think
It becomes
Extinct
When it Blinks.

*

Does an Ood
Refuse its food
When it's up
to no good?

*

When a Judoon
FO-BO-SO
BO-GO-NO-SO-
PO-PO-DO-MA-HO.

*

What happens when
A Quark
Barks in the dark?
Do the other Quarks hark?

*

And really does
A Yeti
Forget where he
Gets his
Spaghetti?

*

And is the Master
Somehow Faster
In a disaster?
(No.)

THE HARD STAIR

(*after* 'Halfway Down')

Halfway down the stairs
is a man
who shouldn't
be.
He whispers sometimes
in my ears
of death
and lonely
nighttime fears.
And what one day
he'll do
to me.

Sometimes I'll be
going up.
And sometimes
I'll be going down.
But he's always
Always

Halfway up the stairs
Waiting with a smile
That's worse than
any frown.

Sometimes I'll forget
if I was going up
or if
I
was
coming down.
That is when
I'll see the man
the man
who shouldn't be.
I hope
and hope
that one day
he won't be me.

A SIMPLE TRUTH

(after 'Lines And Squares')

Avoid the lines, tread in the squares
Or else *They*'ll catch you unawares
To escape their dread designs
Tread on the squares, and not the lines.

But real life is not so simple
Evil does not follow principle
Not all monsters lurk in corners
Squares and lines aren't there to warn us.

Rules I think are just distractions
The greatest evil is inaction.
Rudeness, hatred and being brash
And, of course, a love of cash.

By all means tread the squares, not the lines
But also remember – do be kind
To those you may not understand
And bear in mind the other hand.

We fear what's past and what's to come
The real villains are a zero sum.
Enjoy the now – confront what's there
And... tread a line and not a square.

THE MASTER'S BEARD

I have a lovely beard
So long and pointy
I think it very
much suits
me.

I have a lovely beard
Very lush you see
I really hope
you do
agree.

I have a lovely beard
It means a lot to me.
Look into my eyes
and obey
obey
me.

THE TOYMAKER

(*after* 'Knights and Ladies')

There is in my old picture book
A page at which I never look.
The toys within all seem to cry
And when I look then so will I.
The playing cards have such sad faces
The Jack, Queen, King and all the Aces.
A dolly and a teddy bear
Sigh and wail in full despair.
Girls and boys all turned to toys
So much joy each life destroys.
They came here and they tried their best
Do have a go, my latest guest.
I put them there, you know, my friend
Not all my games have happy ends.
What's that? You think I'd let them out?
Their snakes were laddered, without a doubt,
So many, many years ago.
Perhaps I might – you never know.
Take care you don't end up the same.
Now – care to try my Trilogic Game…?

GOODBYES

Jamie, Zoe and I
Don't like to say our goodbyes.

Once we've saved your isotopes,
Or given poor fish people hopes,
Returned Himalaya's Holy Ghanta,
Or proved there are such things as Macra,
Wonders worked with static electricity,
Or sadly blown up your ancient city,
Driven Yeti out of Covent Garden,
Secured for Mercury miners a pardon,
Say we've saved the Moonbase with a tea-tray,
Taught logicians to open tombs my way,
(You know this is making me giddy!)

Imagine I've misdirected Krotons,
Or baffled Quarks with misplaced protons,
And captured double evil space pirates,
Or my Mexican twin (like me, but irate),
And yes, once we've thwarted angry seaweed,
Met Ann Travers and gone weak-kneed,
Fired deadly rockets from the Wheel In Space,
Gone to meet myself with another face,
(Lots of velvet, lack of grace)

34

And we've banished the Great Intelligence,
Nixed Dominators gaining eminence,
Managed to hold back another Ice Age,
Dealt with the Emperor Dalek's great rage,
Arrested the shape shifters at Gatwick,
Stopped Zaroff (he laid it on a bit thick),
And taught the Daleks how to play at trains,
While Cybermen fiddled about in drains,
Forced an end to all war, gone on the run,
And yes, called home and put a stop to fun,
Well, once we've done all that and a bit more too…

We'll be off.

THE
FLOWER
SOUR

(after 'Daffowdowndilly')

She had a yellow smiling face
Her stem was brightest green
She turned it to the human race
And quivered with a sheen
She blew them deadly kisses
And smothered all with plastic
They perished by the thousand
Their deaths were quite traumatic
But still she wore her smiling face
And her stem of pure Nestene.

THE
COMPANION'S
LAMENT

(*after* 'Independence')

I never really cared for
> "Don't run that way."

I pursed my lips at
> "Follow what I say."

I wasn't a fan of
> "Tell the guard you're ill."

I was frankly tired by
> "Stand very still."

I never liked
> "You wouldn't understand."

I rather frowned at
> "Hush now, hold my hand."

I was not okay with
> "I'll explain later."

Or
> "It's a Tissue Compression Eliminator."

Then there was the rotten
> "There's no time for why."

And the awful
> "Goodbye, my friend, goodbye."

WINNING

Peoples of the universe
Attend please carefully
I am the Master
And I rule eternally.

I shall visit all the planets
And every galaxy
I'll label every comet
It all belongs to me.

You may call me Master
(I'm not fussy 'bout the *The*)
Just look into my eyes
Obey and worship me.

At last I've gone and done it
I own both stars and sea
I'll make all kings and gods
Bow down on bended knee.

We'll have just heaps of meetings
With proposals and decrees
They'll give me all their riches
And hon'rary degrees.

I'll never find it boring
I'll rule them all with glee
But I wonder when the Doctor
Will put a stop to me?

"Peoples of the universe
Listen please to me.
For I am the Doctor
And I'd love a cup of tea."

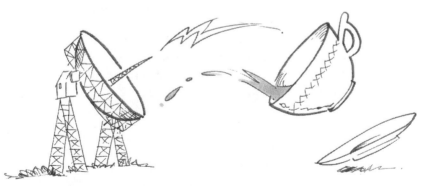

SAID ALICE

(*after* 'Buckingham Palace')

They're changing guard at Rassilon's Palace
Romanadvoratrelundar went down with Alice.
The young Time Lady should be on her guard.
"I think your name is terrible hard,"
                                        Said Alice.

They're changing guard at Rassilon's Palace
Romanadvoratrelundar went down with Alice.
She'd surely never met that girl before.
"Ooh, look a dainty marble floor!"
                                        Said Alice.

They're changing guard at Rassilon's Palace
Romanadvoratrelundar went down with Alice.
Being caught in a time loop's a terrible thing.
"A moment's respite before the reset swing,"
                                        Said Alice.

They're changing guard at Rassilon's Palace
Romanadvoratrelundar went down with Alice.
"Something's breached the transduction barrier!"
"Romana, you're just a terrible worrier,"
                                        Said Alice.

They're changing guard at Rassilon's Palace
Romanadvoratrelundar went down with Alice.
"You're nothing but a psychovore!"
"I've escaped here from a terrible war,"
                                        Said Alice.

They're changing guard at Rassilon's Palace
Romanadvoratrelundar went down with Alice.
"I'm eating this planet minute by minute
Until you're dust and there's nothing in it,"
                                        Said Alice.

They're changing guard at Rassilon's Palace
Romanadvoratrelundar went down with Alice.
Romanadvoratrelundar went down with Alice.
"Just what are you doing?"
                                        Said Alice.

They're changing guard at Rassilon's Palace
Romanadvoratrelundar went down with Alice.
"I'm breaking the loop and throwing you out
To bring your defeat
My poem's not neat
And some of my rhymes
Are terrible crimes
But it should form a reasonable basis
For rupturing a chronic hysteresis,"

       Said Romana.

"Some people should not be allowed near poetry,"

       Said Alice.

"Also, noooooooooooooo!"

       Said Alice.

They're changing guard at Rassilon's Palace
Romanadvoratrelundar went down with... "Oh."
"Something wrong?" "I don't think so."
The Doctor said, "Well, it looks like snow.

       Who's Alice?"

THE HAPPY BRIG

Alistair Gordon Lethbridge Stewart
Had saved the world and this time he knew it.

It wasn't the Doctor (He was on Mars)
It wasn't Ms Shaw (She was playing with jars)
It hadn't been Ms Grant (For she'd been late)
And, due to a cold, it wasn't Mike Yates.
And of course, we really should mention
It hadn't, oh hadn't, been Sgt Benton.

Gordon Alistair Lethbridge Stewart
Had saved the world and this time he knew it.

The PM had not taken his call
Word had spread throughout Whitehall.
They'd made excuses in Geneva
"Perhaps a touch of dengue fever?"
The game was up, they began to fear
It was all in the hands of the Brigadier.

Lethbridge Alistair Gordon Stewart
Had saved the world and this time he knew it.

It wasn't with bullets (they never worked)
He didn't use nanites (they always lurked)
It wasn't a bomb (though they were a blast)
He didn't lay on a chopper (they were too fast)
He could never rely on nuclear
Nor set hands on a trusty bazooka

Alistair Lethbridge Gordon Stewart
Had saved the world and this time he knew it.

It may be laying it on a touch too thick
But it was honestly nothing ballistic
He just strode out to the UFO
With a cheery smile and a fond hello.
"Terribly sorry, you've got the wrong date
This world won't be conquered by a feller who's late."
Don't tangle with Earth or you'll be made fools
By a chap who obeys the Queensbury rules.

Alistair Gordon Lethbridge Stewart
Had saved the world and this time he knew it.

TO ANONYMOUS

I've 100 words a minute
And not one of them's for you.
You're a thing I can't describe
Don't know your what or why or who.
You're an itch I'm not meant to scratch
A take-a-way unordered,
A song that doesn't come on shuffle,
A shopping trip afforded,
The answer to my horoscope.

"Strangers are friends you've not yet met,"
It says so in my magazine
Along with Katie's Diet Secrets,
Psychic poodles and Sudoku,
Plus a girl whose husband minced her.
All human life's therein – but mine.
"You've got it all!" – I'm not convinced.

I'm not seeking tall, dark and handsome
More sort of wiry, sort of lanky.
No muscled Sven, no hirsute Barry
Just suited with a pocket hanky.
The missing bit in my life's sky.
No lover – just that best, best friend
It's your name carried on their heart
They're your laugh, your mate, your end.*
*We all deserve one of these (except for Nerys)

You're one more bus that I've just missed
Like when there's aliens arriving
And I'm on safari, karaoke,
A hen night, or scuba diving.
I've skipped a page in my life's book
Some brilliant's missing from my history
I guess we all feel that, I guess
And yet it's so my mystery.

A stone I saw in a museum
"Grandad! It's me – in Ancient Rome!"
And it was, I'm so sure it hurt.
"Is it, luv? It's late. Let's go home."
Like there's something I'm not being told
A locked door's in my memory.
Something's gone and gone for good
In a life of mist and rain and grey
I cannot put my finger on
Why they'd take my sunny day.

A film without a car explosion
A year without December
Beckham in a bunny onesie
The shape of just can't remember.
You're that one trick that mothers know
Terms and conditions, PPI
That lucky thousandth visitor
You're what's missing – Life's Big Why.

Seeking the best friend I'll never know
I give up. I always do.
I've a hundred words a minute
And not one of them for you.

CURTAIN

(*after* 'Brownie')

At the end of time there is a great big curtain
Something lies behind it, but I don't know who.
I'm sure it's there but I'm not quite certain.
It may be imagination – in which case whose?
One day I went and looked behind the curtain
But I went and there was no thing there
God or monster, no-one said "How do you do?"
But there's something waiting of that I'm sure
And I know that one day it'll say "Boo!"

THE FIVE DOCTORS

(*after* 'The Three Foxes')

Once upon a time there were five little Doctors
They went to Gallifrey and frankly they shocked her.
One got lost along the way in a temporal fracture
The rest went to the Dead Zone and a secret unlocked-er.
They faced off against dastard interlocutors,
Scrambled entry coders while time tick-tocked-er.
Thwarted Cybermen and an agent provocateur
Escaped from mad Yeti and a Raston Robot-er.
They dodged mind probes from a vengeful chief proctor,
They ate dainty pineapple and knocked out the Master,
Read Old High Gallifreyan and roared with laughter,
They unmasked the President and cunning impostors,
Then escaped quickly. And Flavia? They mocked her.
A wilder story you could not concocter
That's all that I know of the five little Doctors.

SOMETHING BORROWED, SOMETHING BLUE

(after 'The Wrong House')

I went into a box and it wasn't a box.
On the inside it was big, on the outside it was small.
And it had a garden
A swimming pool
A library
It wasn't like a box at all.

I went into a box and it wasn't a box.
It had no shelves, just a great big hall.
And it had some snowmen
And kitchens
And wardrobes
It wasn't like a box at all.

I went into a box and it wasn't a box.
It had lots of rooms for nothing at all.
And it had corridors.
And butterflies.
And galleries.
It wasn't like a box at all.

I went into a box and it wasn't a box.
I asked it who owned it and it smiled.
It said no-one owned it.
No-one.
No-one
No-one owned that box at all.

I went into a box and it wasn't a box.
I asked the box to go wandering.
We could go to planets
We could visit stars
Or Tuesday.
That box could go anywhere at all.

And so we did.

THE
GUARDIANS

Creation has two Guardians
One is Black and one is White
One's for when things go too wrong
And one's for when they go too right.

"The problem is," the White One said,
"Every day I'm rushed off my feet –
Evil, plague, famine, war, untold dead
Life's such a mess – it's just not neat."

"I'm fine with that," the Black One said
"It makes my life so simple
There's knitting, jigsaws, baking bread,
Hobbies help to fill my time – it's ample."

"That's the point, my dear old friend,"
Said White – "Things they could be neater
Let's bring this division to an end
(And thank you for the sweater)."

"Oh dear," the Black One shut his book
His face was not so rosy.
"To draw a line, how bad that'll look,
Just when I'm getting cosy."

"I call upon the Key To Time
To bring about some balance!" cried White
"An end to chaos, mess and crime?"
Sighed Black, "Say I've not got that right!

"Fine, well fine, for this I've planned
Your tiresome schemes I'll thwart
Has White a champion in mind?
I hope you've given it some thought."

"There's one I trust the Key to find,
The Time Lord called the Doctor.
They say he has a brilliant mind…
Oh –" The White Guard spoke to laughter.

THE BOY WONDER

I'm very good at maths
So why does no-one like me?
It doesn't add up
(That's a joke, I'm good at those).
I'm cleverer than anybody else
But no-one seems to care.
I am so bright.
It's just not fair.
I do times tables in my bed at night.
Ask me a square root, I'm sure to know
And I've all the fun primes to hand
I know pi to that nth degree
And Fibonacci's not a mystery
And yet, and yet, the sadness is
That great as numbers are,
They're just not friends.

STEPS

I love that fresh new planet smell
A world untrodden – it's so swell
Just over that mountain
Or across that plain
Adventure is waiting.
Beyond that fenced-off gating.

Stay Off The Grass! Keep Out!
Intruders Will Be Shot!
Top Secret! Look, Just Stay Away!
Ah.
  My feet shall bend your way.

What's around that deadly corner?
Last words from a mourner?
A city in rubble?
An old friend in trouble?
Bonkers mad-eyed priests?
Invites to their feasts?
Helpful slave girls to charm?
Kings to rescue from harm?
Ancient curses to lift?
Fallen girders to shift?
Famous names to drop?
Lethal countdowns to stop?
(I love it when they get to 001)
It's all just such fun.

Each world's a fresh blank page
I admit – it's my stage.
And it all starts – I cannot hide
With that first
                step
                        outside.

THE RED AND THE BLUE

(*after* 'The Dormouse and the Doctor')

There once was a Dormouse who lived in a shed
As battle raged between loyalists (blue) and rebels (red)
And all day long he'd a wonderful view
Of victories (red) and triumphs (blue).

A Doctor came hurrying past and he cried:
"Good grief little friend, how come you've survived?
What with all the massacres and bombs and whatnot?
Well, it seems dear chap, you've been luckily forgot."

The Dormouse winced at his view and sadly replied
"But can't you stop it?" "Oh, I've tried and I've tried,"
The Doctor he vowed, "I've used charm and persuasions,
I've even faked up an alien invasion."

"But red and blue really want to wipe out each other,
Cities, families, mother against mother
They can't even agree on what they're fighting for
They just thirst for more, more of this stupid, stupid war."

"It's said," ventured the Dormouse, "It began in Heaven,
Great battles among giants raging in the skies.
What's happening here is just poison in the well
As those arguing gods turn creation into Hell."

The Doctor he sighed. "You're well informed for a mouse,
Permit me to suggest a lovely change of house.
My ship's over there, we shall reach it with ease
And I promise you it offers just roomfuls of cheese."

The Doctor and the Dormouse, they went their sad way
And left battle behind them without further say.
Bombardments, and screams, oh the two sides they skirmished
Plenty of atrocities (blue) and victories (red).

And so the planet fell, its life force at an end
But at last, at least, the Doctor had made a new friend.

THE MARA

Into the woods went the girl.
She knew mother didn't want it, so.
"Shall we talk?" said the snake.
"But I'm a good little girl. No!"

"I fear we will," smiled the snake.
"Are you really so very good?
That's not what I think
Or why would you walk in the wood?"

The little girl did not reply.
"Life is full of reasons Not To,
Don't Touch and Don't Ask Why.
This is where I agree with you."

"But my chick, it doesn't have to be
Just hold out your hand and
Look at me.
                 Look at me.
And each other we'll understand
Splendidly.
                 No, look at me.
Look
       At
          Me."

The young girl came out of the woods
                 Eventually
And her mother she was waiting.
"What's This? How dare you disobey!"
She was really shouting.
"Good girls know not to go that way!"

"Why just look at your knees
Bad things happen to girls
Who climb up trees!
And what have you done to your curls?

"There's monsters lurking in those woods
I warned you for a reason
I want to keep you good
Innocence is a short season.

"My sweet, you are in quite a state
Let's clean you up 'fore you go wild."
"Mother you're too late,"
And then the hungry girl, she smiled.

SHORTNESS
OF BREATH

Tainted Love and chips,
Sunshine on her lips,
Red wine and Women Wept,
Pass the port Harriet,
Amazing ears, lopsided grin,
Always feeling the Earth's spin,
Vinegar and bananas,
Captain Jack's Pyjamas,
England in the Blitz,
High tea at the Ritz,
Kronkburger and Pajatas,
Genghis Khan and Blue Peter.
One brave weather balloon,
Poor old Moxx of Balhoon.
Lynda with a Y
Jackie Tyler's shepherd's pie.
Even Auton Plastic
These things are fantastic.

Coleslaw and pickled onions,
Zombies in Cardiff dungeons.
Cassandra, Metaltron,
Dickens left the gas on.
Bad Wolf or Dalek Scheme
Are you my Repeated Meme?
The Mighty Jagrafess,
Adam's weird new face,
The Emperor Dalek's fleet
And my two left feet.
Bad Wolf and Clive's Shed
Those walking undead.
Perfect Brides and Nestenes
Over-active nanogenes.
Slitheen romancing
Have we done dancing?
The fear of the loner
Never going to Barcelona.
Surviving war galactic
These things are not fantastic.

Fantastic or not
They all meant

A lot.

ODE TO A
KRYNOID

(*after* Pooh's Good Hum)

The more it snows
      (Diddley-dum)
The more it grows
      (Diddley-dum)
The more it goes
      (Diddley-dum)
On killing.

And nobody knows
      (Diddley-dum)
As it flowers
      (Diddley-dum)
And it devours
      (Diddley-dum)
If there's a way
      (Diddley-dum)
Of it stopping.
      (Oo-ee-ooo)

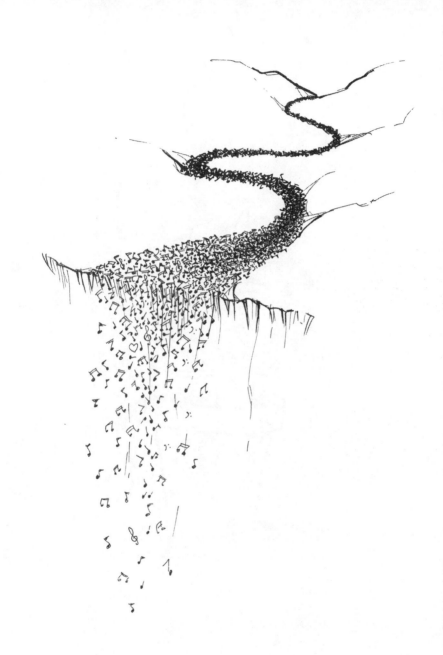

TO HER
COY DOCTOR

Had we but world enough and time,
This coyness, Doctor, were no crime.
We would sit down, and think which way
To turn the pace of our love's day.
But that, alas, will never do
For I well, my love, know you.

Or else we'd sail on time's tides
Fighting love's war 'pon both sides
Me quicksilver'd like a Rutan
You steadfast as Sontaran –
I'd be slick of wit, sylph of form
You like a grape in Benidorm.

Our loves approach from diff'rent routes
Yours often tangled where mine shoots.
My heart falls for each shifting face
As you grow wise and tall in grace
No mind which course our bodies send
A Library's where we start and end.

Our middle's where we most agree
A muddle's what the others see.
True, though I do kill you at the start
It's you who bore me through the heart.
Sometimes we blaze like Perseids
I shout your love from Pyramids.

Others, you've aeons to say your love
But would rather talk about your glove,
Its touch doubtless tender, but still
Leaves not a smudge on windowsill.
You tread time and leave no traces
Beyond a truce twixt warring races.

Though my dear holds me in prison
One touch frees me with oblivion.
From the crash of the Byzantium
To the towers of Derilium
Our race is one long arc of fun
For some it's just a Demon's Run.

I'd give my age to your every part
And the last breath should speak your heart.
I'd chase you cross Mutter's Spiral
I'll make our love nano-viral
No matter where it is you hide
My path draws me 'ventually to your side.

Remember this most certainly
That feelings fill eternity
For at my back I always hear
Your blue box roaring near.
And yonder all behind us lie
Seas of wasted opportunity.

Give up my love, give in to fate
It's sometimes not the girl who waits.
Let's forget for once our duty
And gather up in arms our beauty
For though our days hold to the sun
It's yet our nights that see us run.

CHRISTMAS
ON MARS

Why does it never snow on Mars?
I'll find it out for my memoirs.
Martians I've met come from when it's cold
I guess they must be jolly old.

Mars has had a change in climate
It all depends on how you time it.
Some find that good, others couldn't be sorrier
Such as, my old chums, the Ice Warriors

Azaxyr, Varga, Sskel, Turoc,
Izlyr, Slaar, Ssorg, Zondal, Skaldak
Fellows of fine noble mettle
Though with names like angry kettles.

No wonder they do hiss and shout
When there's so little ice about
It's one thing when with the stars you've warred
To come back and find your home world's thawed

Perhaps it's only time who really knows
Why on Mars it never snows.

SKIPPING SONG

(*after* 'Hoppity')

Hippity-hoppity
To the shoppity
Goes Jackie Tyler!

Hoppity-skippity
From the market
Jackie comes home.

The phone it has not rung.
The phone it has not rung.
Is her daughter still alive?
Hoppity-hop!

* * *

Bouncity-bounce
Through space
Falls Katarina

Gaspity-gasp
Struggling to breathe
Poor Katarina

Will her god rescue her?
Will her god rescue her?
Well, gods like sacrifice
Sighs Katarina.

* * *

Whizzity-whizzity-whirr
To the Conversion Chamber
Goes Yvonne Hartman

Buzzity-buzzity-slice
The drills aren't quite nice
Thinks Yvonne Hartman

I did my duty
I did my duty
Oh god.

* * *

THE
GALACTIC
COUNCIL

Twelve men went to mow
Went to mow down all creation
A badger and a Christmas Tree
And one was called Celation.

Twelve men went to mow
Went to mow down all creation
A badger and a Christmas Tree
And one they called Celation.
With the help of Mavic Chen
And a full emm of Taranium
They went to mow down all creation.

Twelve men went to mow
Went to mow down all creation
A badger and a Christmas Tree
And one they called Celation.
Plus Malpha, Beaus, Warrien
Then Sentreal with Mavic Chen
And PS that full emm of Taranium
They went to mow down all creation.

Twelve men went to mow
Went to mow down all creation
A badger and a Christmas Tree
And one they called Celation.
Plus Malpha, Beaus, Warrien
And Sentreal, and Mavic Chen
With Trantis, Monsieur Gearon,
Plus don't forget that full emm of Taranium
They went to mow down all creation.

Twelve men went to mow
Went to mow down all creation
A badger and a Christmas Tree
And one they called Celation.
Plus Malpha, Beaus, Warrien
And Sentreal, magic Mavic Chen
Jane Trantis, groovy Gearon,
AND the Fifth Galaxy's Zephon,
(Sadly having to give it a miss
Was the Embodiment Gris).
And you won't forget that full emm of Taranium!
They went to mow down all creation

I think that's nearly all
The members of that delegation
(But we can never be quite sure
Due to archival obliteration)
But

    (one more time)

              There's a badger, a Christmas Tree
And one they called Celation.
Plus Malpha, Beaus, Warrien
And Sentreal, then Mavic Chen,
With Trantis, oh and Gearon,
Plus the Fifth Galaxy's Zephon,
And never ever forget that full emm of Taranium.
This lot went to mow down all creation.

They were good to go,
That lethal delegation
But when they went to mow,
Went to mow down all creation
The Daleks they didn't know
And met total Extermination!

JOSEPHINE GRANT

(after 'Jonathan Jo')

Jo Jo Grant
Had a mouth like an "oh!"
And a life full of surprises.

Although she joined UNIT quite inchoate
She soon sailed on seas of giant maggots
She met ever so many savages,
Turned down simply heaps of marriages,
While stopping muddy worlds being colonised
She was very frequently hypnotised.
She was sacrificed at a syzygy,
Passed screaming through a singularity,
She didn't once, despite the Doctor's ego,
Reverse polarity of neutron flow.

She did enjoy Captain Yates' romancing
Till he sadly took her Morris dancing.
She so adored the Brigadier's moustache
Even when he talked such balderdash.
She stole the heart of a Draconian
And honeymooned upon the Amazon.
She parachuted from an icecano
And called her grandson Santiago.
For vile villains she never gave two figs
And laughed at those silly gnashing Drashigs.
At those weird fiendish experimenters
She just smiled on her many adventures.
(Though she never met a pterodactyl
To say other would be counterfactual)
A scream with laughs she'd sometimes intersperse
Because Jo Grant saw the whole universe.

Miss Jo Grant
Never said "shan't"
That's why she won all life's prizes.

A GOOD MAN

Good men take the long way round,
It goes with the higher ground,
Keeping sacred noble vows,
And really searing eyebrows.

Good men should sound quite Scottish
Helps with being stand-offish
Suggests you'll win any fight
Just by being profoundly right.

Good men should have a careful plan
Which they'll (like this rhyme) ignore
They're always ten moves ahead
Their feet most firmly planted.

Good men don't plan their breakfast
In eggs and jam they're reckless
But long ago they had a hunch
There's no such thing as a free lunch.

Good men choose with whom to trifle
(No chance if you own that rifle)
They work hard, they don't forget
And they don't lose – well, not yet.

Good men never toss a pawn
They'd rather eat a Janis Thorn
What good's that one true friend
If they're not with you at the end?

Good men they don't surrender
Even if the bill's a spender.
Losing's not a cost to swallow
They'll be back tomorrow.

And tomorrow, tomorrow
And all the days that follow.
They'll get you back, no mind the cost
Because to them a friend's not lost.

Good men they take the long way round
It goes with all that higher ground.

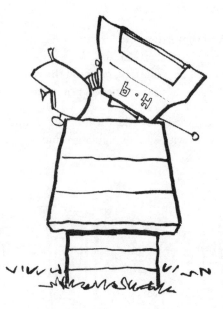

THE GUIDE DOG

I like to let him cheat at chess
I love to answer No with Yes
My rules are simple and also true
Without doubt they'd apply to you.
I always answer Negative
Or perhaps Affirmative.

Why answer in one syllable?
Brevity is just risible.
Be governed by always being right
It affords your listeners quiet delight
If not, answer Negative
Or just perhaps Affirmative.

I will admit I'm no good at slopes
Sand, stairs and mud are just nopes.
I regret my lack of battery power
But a lot can be done in an hour.
It's why I prefer Affirmative
To a bold cold solid Negative.

He forgives my failings with puddles
Because I sort out his frightful muddles
As our little song draws to an end
A robot dog's always your best friend.
And that's never Negative
It's definitely Affirmative.

RASSILON WHY?

(after 'Cottleston Pie')

Rassilon, Rassilon, Rassilon Why?
A man should die, but this man shan't die
Ask me a riddle and I'll reply
Rassilon, Rassilon, Rassilon Why?

Rassilon, Rassilon, Rassilon Why?
Gallifrey rises and so do I
Ask me a riddle and I'll reply
Rassilon, Rassilon, Rassilon Why?

Rassilon, Rassilon, Rassilon Why?
Immortality's a curse, I don't know why
Ask me a riddle and I'll reply
Rassilon, Rassilon, Rassilon Why?

Rassilon, Rassilon, Rassilon Why?
There's one rule for you, and one for me
I wouldn't want us to disagree
Rassilon, Rassilon, Rassilon Why?

YETI SONG

Sing Ho! For the life of a Yeti!
Sing Ho! You're jealous I bet-ty!
I don't much mind if the world disappears
Cos my furry belly is full of spheres

Telling me to obey, obey, obey
I don't much care if it snows or thaws
Cos I've such a lot of blood on my lovely paws!
Slashing and maiming, slaughtering my way.

Sing Ho! For the life of a Yeti!
Sing Ho! You're jealous I bet-ty!
Now everyone's dead I'm coming for you!

COOL THING

I do so like my lovely tie,
You're jealous. Ask me why?
It's a bow bow tie
That's just why
A red bow tie.
It has a shape
That is clever
It folds in
On itself
& Out forever
A Möbius loop
For a nincompoop
I'll confess to be sly
Bows are tricky to tie.
The start and ending are nigh
I do so like my lovely tie.

GAMES

I am so very terribly good at games
It doesn't help that I'm bad at names
But sit down stranger, let's draw out the board
And see our eternal chess game scored.

Where were we? You pick'd black and I took white
And settled in for an age-old fight
We battled from Silk Road to Araby
And, dear sir, you always return to me.

Sometimes I take your pieces, you take mine
It's no hardship, the game is fine.
As the ages fall, our contest continual
Glaciers creep and mountains fall.

There's no ending but mine, Time Lord
You say you're thinking, I say you're bored.
One day I'll win, and then you'll see –
What playing a friend means to me.

Your move, dear sir, your move.

ABSENCES

(*after* 'Before Tea')

Miss Clara
Has not been seen
For more than a week. She slipped inside
The stationery cupboard. Surely not to hide?
We all went looking for her. Miss Clara?
Where are yer?

Miss? Miss?
What is this?
We've got big exams at the end of term
If you go missing then how can we learn?
Also, the Head's cross. You've gone too far, Miss.

Miss Clara
Slipped back in the
Middle of a lesson. "Now, where were we?"
"*Where were you?!?*" "What's the hurry?
I've been in space, met Ghandi for curry,
Saved the human race, s'okay don't worry
And no, don't thank me."
Oh Miss Clara
Miss, this time
You've gone too far-er.

POSSIBILIES

(after 'Cherry Stones')

Tinker, Tailor
Soldier, Sailor
Rich Man, Poor Man
Beggarman, Thief

These are the many lives to see
In the stones of my sweet cherry tree.

But what about a Physicist,
Thinker, Slayer
Eternal Sailor
Gell Guard,
Or Nano Biologist?
What about the Vanir or a Tharil at the Gate?
What about a Malin or Giant Spider's Mate?
What about a Policeman looking in the junkyard?
Or the circumlocuting, prosecuting Valeyard?
What about a Vervoid voiding Thrematologist?
Or an ever over-eager radiation physicist?
What about a blood-thirsty Lord High Priestess
Or a pluckily unlucky air hostess?
Don't forget a fiddler with rat genetics
Or an emotionless abuser of cybernetics

There are more lives to see
Than there are stones on Metebelis Three

RICE PUDDING

Unlimited rice pudding, temporal ghosts
Bus stations, cruelty and burnt toast
These are the things I don't like the most.

Fascism, idiocy, a waffling bore
Old gods, sideways villains, the Earth's core
These are things I find terrible chores.

Recursive occlusions, rips in Time's skin,
Lost luggage, cold porridge, worlds wearing thin
These are all the things I declare grim.

Liquorice, apricots, opening night,
Sudden triumph, old friends, a fair fight
These are things in which I take delight.

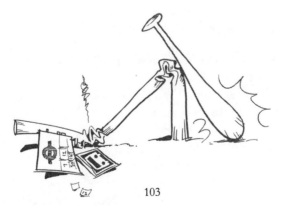

HAVE YOU SEEN....?

Whatever became of Perpugilliam Brown?
She's let her whole family down
She said she was off backpacking
Seems she was a victim of bizarre kidnapping.
Whatever became of Perpugilliam Brown?

Her mother (it's said) has begun to frown
(Quite ruining her surgeon's reknown).
She'd a university place
Instead she's larking off in space!
Whatever became of Perpugilliam Brown?

You know I've heard she's run off with a clown
Who calls himself by a proper noun!
Her step-dad he is so distraught
He's searching the docks till she's caught.
Whatever became of Perpugilliam Brown?

She nearly died stopping a mutant drown,
I know, poor girl, such a letdown!
But she'd planned for a botanist
Not a career, yet she would insist.
Whatever became of Perpugilliam Brown?

By now she should be living downtown
Not stopping nuclear meltdown
Or saving us from a fireball
Noble I know, but is that all?
Whatever became of Perpugilliam Brown?

Not to gossip, but it's all over town
She's set her cap at a man with a crown!
What was wrong with an accountant?
Not some alien militant!
Breeding will out, it's always shown.
Well, look what became of Perpugilliam Brown!

NEXT
EPISODE

"Kill them! Kill them now!"
Well yes, but how?

Is it with a gun?
(There's always one!)

What about a flute?
(That would be a hoot)

Push me in a pit!
(Are you sure I'll fit?)

Here's my robot twin!
(Where shall I begin?)

Offer me to god?
(That's a little odd)

Throw me into space?
(I'll keep a straight face)

Turn me into stone?
(That one's not unknown)

Restart the big bang?
(Ooh, that's quite the thang)

Shrink me into dust?
(Well now, if you must)

Call for the Daleks?
(Won't see me for parsecs)

Turn me to compost?
(Well now, I'm engrossed)

Tell them my real name?
(The internet's aflame)

Ah, a fit of pique?
(I'll be back next week)

See, no matter how
You say "Kill them now!"

I assure you, friend
It won't be <u>MY</u> end.

HARRIET JONES, PM

(*after* 'Journey's End')

"Don't you think she looks tired?"
Do forgive me, I'm rather wired!
Earth's in danger, then? Again?
Send for Harriet Jones, PM!

This world we shall defend
My poor alien friends.
Fear my network subwave
Earth from you I'll save!

From cottage hospitals,
And nasty windbag fools,
Even alien blackmail.
I've saved us without fail.

Daleks, please have no doubt
I'll gladly sort you out.
Now, before it all turns sour
This'll be my finest hour.
Harriet Jones, PM out.

FRIEND SHIP

Susan, Barbara and Ian
Vicki, Dodo and Steven.

Ben, Polly, Jamie
Victoria and Zoe.

Liz, Jo and Sarah
Harry, Brig and Leela.

Romanadvoratrelundar
And K-9 (the dog wonder).

Adric, Nyssa, Tegan
Turlough and Kamelion.

Peri and Melanie
Ace (aka Dorothy).

Rose, Jack and Jackie
Martha, (horse) and Mickey.

Donna, Donna, Donnaaaa!
(Never forgetting her)

Amy, Winston, Rory
River (that's another story).

Clara, Oswin, Clara
Oswald, Osgoods, Clara.

(Also, Clara, Clara, and more Clara
Never got the end of that palaver)

Then Nardole, Bill and River too
And,
    MOST IMPORTANTLY
          There's
              YOU.

AFTERWORDS

Sunset came to the Thousand Year Wood. It had been
a lovely long day, and, although Figment hadn't yet met
the mysterious Officer Sandcars, he'd had such a lot of
interesting adventures along the way.

"Maybe my call was just not urgent," he thought
philosophically to himself. "Exciting as new friends no
doubt are," said Figment, "there's something even better
about spending time with old ones."

He waved goodbye to his friends Whoot and Bigger,
marvelling that they had, after all, caught a Gallifrump.
He wondered if it would still be there tomorrow. Perhaps
not. Ah well. Never mind. They could always catch it again.

His footsteps took him back in the direction of the strange
blue tree. Only it wasn't where he had left it. Things never
were, not in Figment's life. Why, often he had trouble
finding his house. But he carried on, not worried by the
darkening sky, or the gathering cold, just looking and
looking for the square blue tree and humming the little
hum that the tree had taught him.

Truth to tell, he spent a little bit longer looking for it than
he should have. Figment suddenly realised that it was

quite dark and, as he'd given the Gallifrump his mittens, his fingers were very cold. In the distance the NightWolves were starting to call to each other, singing their song about how much they liked eating Figments.

"Oh dear," said Figment, feeling very worried.

He ran on, hoping that his footsteps were taking him home.

But they were not. He was in a darkly dark bit of the Thousand Year Wood. And he could tell that the NightWolves were ever so close now.

"I am a very silly Figment," said Figment crossly to himself.

Which was when he turned a corner.

Now, he should have realised that something was Up, as, strictly speaking, forests do not have corners. But turn a corner he did, and then he realised that all was well.

For standing right there was the strange blue tree, looking all new and bright.

Better still, there was snow in the night sky.

Leaning against the blue tree was that best thing of all, the oldest of old friends.

"Jonathan Smith, you've come back to the Thousand Year Wood!" Figment cried. As he said the words, he felt a little shiver inside. He was so pleased to see his friend, but also worried – because sometimes the arrival of Jonathan Smith meant an end, not a beginning.

Figment looked fearfully up at Jonathan Smith.

And Jonathan Smith smiled and Figment knew that it was all going to be much more than all right.

"You called?" said Jonathan Smith with a smile as warm as a Christmas fireplace. "Shall we go?"

"But where?" said Figment, his little hearts giddy.

"Oh, somewhere," said Jonathan Smith. "Eventually."

*

So away they went somewhere – but whenever they go and whatever happens to them along the way, that was only their beginning.

In the magical heart of the Thousand Year Wood, upon the footsteps of Figment and his oldest friend, it will always, always be snowing.

VERITY

Young Verity went to the BBC
It was full of Men Who Knew What To Do
"Young girl, have you come to make us all tea?"
"No, I'm the Producer of Doctor Who."

"What's this?" laughed the Men. "What can you know?
"Don't worry your head with old Doctor Who.
Why's a sweet girl going near a sci-fi show?
It's grown-up stuff. There's nice typing to do."

Young Verity smiled and she stood her ground.
"I know what I'm doing, thank you so much,
Leave it with me and I'll bring you all round.
I'll think you'll find I've got the common touch."

Verity got her way (she always did),
Cavemen, Daleks, Aztecs, Marco Polo
The kids loved it andthe Men felt stupid
"That girlie's just lucky – she doesn't know!"

She faced each day's battles with a brand new hat
As she sailed past those boys' giggling glares
"I just tell myself they're looking at that!"
And she trotted right through them up the stairs

Said the Men: "Verity, luv, you've had a blast."
(Cos the TARDIS went on, and on she flew)
"But this kiddie show, how long can it last?"
And Verity winked. Because, well, she knew.